A Celestial Message

Erastus C. Gaffield

Contents

A Celestial Message

BY

Erastus C. Gaffield

INTRODUCTION.

In the first conditions of his life upon earth, man was unable to perceive the possible evolution of a higher correspondence of spirit in consciousness; the subtle laws which obtained in the spiritual spheres were not realized. He received no conscious revelations from celestial sources, nor did he perceive what destiny held in store for his race, nor what would be its part in a world of cosmic, and, apparently, antithetical forces. He had but very limited, if any, conception of his inherent, natural, spiritual powers. He had learned little or nothing of nature, nor knew that its laws were subject to exploitation, through researches for which only he possessed the latent capacity of organization and pursuit.

It has required many centuries of wars, struggles, famines, disease, and other educational forces to enable him to even imperfectly realize his relation and responsibility to the law, under which he incarnated and went forth, a free moral agent, into a world of an infinite number and variety of undeveloped resources.

Yet above all other creations of Infinite Love he was to be the most important factor, the only intelligent exponent of the universal life. His spiritual origin antedates all conception and measure of time. Notwithstanding the lapse of unnumbered centuries, since his first appearance upon earth, his present imperfect knowledge of his real environments, and often his inability to correctly perceive the meaning of the spiritual laws with which his own destiny is so intimately related, are both unitary and collective evidence, that in the evolutionary progress of his soul to its final complete mastery of all conditions and states he has still much to accomplish, many imperfections to correct, before he will attain to the state of perfect harmony. Yet from age to age he has progressively unfolded an increasing capacity of analysis and reason.

Through the intuitions and in consciousness also he has, in recent times, realized in a larger ratio, than in any of the earlier periods of his earth existence, such progress as distinctly indicates his deific origin, and that he will accomplish the conquest of self, the final, sublime victory.

Though a limited unit of force, often incorrectly manifesting reason, intuition, perception, ideality, and other allied attributes of the soul, he has so far advanced toward the accomplishment of his destiny that he now receives impressions which are indeed the foregleams of a spiritual apotheosis.

At the commencement of this century he is probably better able than at any preceding time, to forecast the intimate affinities which will, in the future, bridge the apparent chasm between the objective and subjective spheres of life.

Certain delicately organized and gifted children of humanity have advanced to a definite and clear realization of the basic principles of divine harmony, received revelations concerning the laws of spiritual vibration, and of other laws relating to the many important issues of life. The sum of all such teachings has superseded, in the consciousness of many, what had before been incorrectly taught about such matters.

Heterodoxy is not now a term of reproach, for he that is accused of heresy knows the truth through personal experience, confidently expects that some time his less informed brother will, through aspiration for the Eternal Good, realize more of truth, beauty and love in the kingdom of spirit He has learned that spiritual wisdom, possible to receive from higher sources, is the natural birthright of every one, though not yet properly valued, nor the means of perfecting its potentialities sufficiently recognized. Such knowledge is the most important factor in the life here, and absolutely necessary for the consummation of harmonial relations hereafter.

In order to realize the soul's aspirations for a constant, progressive unfoldment, the teachings of the higher thought movement could be profitably adopted as part of the curriculum in all educational institutions, especially in the leading universities of the world, and be made obligatory in all post-graduate courses.

The larger contributors to such causes may well seek the higher inspiration when dictating the uses to which their benefactions shall be applied. The world's great teachers of other times, with knowledge increased by later experiences and observation, will, I am quite convinced, gladly co-operate in such promotions, when those entrusted to lead others shall have advanced to correspondences that permit the influx of wisdom from spheres where truth is the law of being.

The subject matter of this little book was received from a source to leave no doubt in the mind of the scribe of its essential correctness, though he, as an instrument, used for its transmission, acknowledges many imperfections, which have doubtless detracted from the perfection of its revelation.

He has tried faithfully to reproduce in their entirety the vibrations of celestial thought as received. When, however, it is understood that all such revelations and the mode of their expressions are in a measure modified and limited by human organism, he trusts the work will receive the indulgent consideration of its readers.

ERASTUS C. GAFFIELD.
BOSTON, 1902.

CHAPTER I.

Several important questions have been asked and variously answered,—such as, "If a man die shall he live again?" "What is truth? " "Show me the Father, and it sufficeth me," and others of like import; while but a few, however, have asked to have the realities of excarnate life shown them or described. No doubt the majority have always believed that the mystery could not be revealed; and the small minority, accepting the facts of spirit intercommunication, have, from various causes, been prevented from receiving in an intelligent manner the information which can be given and can be usefully applied to the moral and intellectual instruction of many. This is the only apology or explanation I desire to offer for attempting that which, as yet, has not been satisfactorily accomplished.

Coming into relation with one not unknown within these latitudes, I realize his willingness to act as an amanuensis in the transmission of such facts as I may be able to impress upon his mind, relative to certain generic conditions of spirit life which will be more fully explained in succeeding chapters. As the higher intelligences never fail and are always identified with success and accomplish all things which they consider advisable to undertake, I, also, shall rely upon them for assistance.

For identification, I will state that several years ago one who was adjudged a student, poet, and philosopher, having worked much for his fellow-men, in the ordinary operations of nature's unchanging law, passed out from his always rather delicate frame, and, after a short time in a semi-conscious condition, awoke to the reality of being. What he has subsequently experienced, observed in others, and learned in various ways during his sojourn in the spirit world, will form the subject matter of this book.

First: The sleep, about which not very much can be said, except that it is an experience, varying in duration, but always sufficiently extended to permit the astral form (which at first develops in weakness, corresponding in many respects to the state of the physical organism at the time of its separation from the spirit), to attract from matter in its various conditions such life forces as the electrical and magnetic elements contain, to enable the spirit to clothe itself and to pass into correspondences which its previous environments, aspirations, spiritual life and consciousness have created for it. Here, then, is practically the starting-point of the soul in its new condition, though the continued and manifested purpose of the Great Oversoul operating through law has not yet been revealed. Its philosophy may have been studied to advantage upon planes of human habitation. The pictures painted by imagination now will either fade altogether, or come into fuller beauty with their value increased a thousand-fold.

In this corridor of the great court, presided over by the inner consciousness, each juror, with ample evidence before him,—unmistakably true and impossible to refute,—individualizes judgment upon his own previous life and prescribes penalties and methods of execution. Nor have such judgments and penalties ever been at variance with justice. Not an instance of appeal, if there be such, in all the eons of eternity. Here is a tribunal without attorneys, except it be as parties in interest, without expense, clients constantly changing, but a single case upon the docket never missed, working with perfect regularity, always dispensing absolute equity!

How is this accomplished?

I confess that at first it seemed to me a marvel, a wondrous arrangement contrived by some illuminated genius peculiar to the spiritual life; but, upon investigation, the matter appeared very simply arranged and perfectly adjusted for objects to be attained. There was not the suggestion or least evidence of revenge.

There was no great white throne, nor any Eternal Judge in propria persona or "by attorney in fact" pronouncing awful dooms upon miscreants; made such partly through inheritances from all the ages, and largely by environments. Nothing of such a sort.

I have spoken of the spirit's semi-conscious state and of attracting to itself from matter an astral covering, a robe, if you so please to call it.

Now there are a good many peculiarities about those robes, which it seems to me perfectly proper and right that I should explain.

How are they formed? Are they all of the same texture? What is their color?

These, and many other questions you may well ask, for every son of earth must wear one in his turn.

Upon entrance to the spirit life he will have no choice in its selection. Previously, while upon earth, he will have exhausted all opportunities, manufactured the fibre, created the loom and woven the web, but perhaps unknown and unconsciously, have also, like water lines in finest tissue of paper or silk, stamped thereon a full and correct record of his principal acts, whether influenced from love or revenge, generosity or hatred, harmony or discord; and the colors of these lines, now brought out with special distinctness, luminous and bright as they may be, or dark, grim, and to the conscious soul, now sensitive to thousands of heretofore unperceived vibrations, horrible to the eye and distinct evidence of shame and dishonor, from which the spirit shrinks in terror. And yet, through the law of attractions and similars, there is for the time no other garment for the humiliated and disgraced spirit.

Imagine a great concourse in your city[1], with which I am familiar, starting from the capitol, headed by the governor and staff, followed by leading military and civic officers and citizens, finally including those in lowest states of physical and moral conditions. You have but a faint picture, rather indefinite and not wholly parallel, for some of those leading in such a procession should perhaps be relegated to the rear, but the contrast will suffice to illustrate the idea.

Here the moral qualities have survived the change, and are represented in colors of beauty. The absence of those attributes, indicating imperfect developments, are also fully expressed.

Each goes to his own plane in that great realm, co-extensive with the universe, and filled with attractions peculiar to and fitting the conditions that his supremacy of desires have created.

This I first observed, and, understanding something of spiritual rewards and penalties, was not surprised, though the practical operation of the law was somewhat different from preconceived ideas upon the subject.

In the great ocean of living thought entities and vibrations upon higher planes than I had ever realized while upon earth, I saw many manifestations of the law, which I had previously, through intuition, perceived as having possible expression;

1   Boston, Mass.

but, in the assumption of their expression, I recalled having suffered severe criticisms of those supposed to know many things.

There were other matters of considerable importance, revealed in these first lessons on the spirit side, that had never been suggested to me, nor do I know that others have upon earth ever received any revelations in regard to them.

I noticed that the excarnated spirit neophytes were under the necessity, or at least so considered themselves, of observing laws relative to hunger and thirst, and with some, this matter seemed to create the greatest consternation and fear.

About them, in great abundance, existed every element, perfectly adapted to the necessities of all; but, in proportion to the moral ignorance and depravity of earthly states, the fear seemed to increase, and consequently the inability to take advantage of the situation. From this cause many, especially those who had enjoyed the rich favors of earth but who never contributed to the personal comfort of others, seemed to suffer the most.

At this point of spiritual experience, contrition—partly resulting from hunger and from other causes also—seemed to be very sincere and absolute. As they could easily read their own records, and every special deed done in the body, no doubt ample reasons were found for the deplorable mental states of those whom I found in such sore distress.

Here let me state that it is not given to those upon the same planes of vibration to fully read the records of others, though the general appearances of robes do plainly and sufficiently indicate that such records are correctly shown.

In this phase of spiritual conditions I was greatly interested; but not fully understanding the methods or established regulations for relief, I could do but very little in ministering to the needs, all too apparent. I had not long to wait, however, for I soon perceived the presence of some to whom authority had been delegated, to minister to those cases then under my particular observation.

I learned that there are schools, presided over by ample corps of competent teachers. Into these schools grown men and women were taken where, beside children and even infants, they were taught the alphabet of spiritual facts. The proud and haughty upon earth—they who in self-sufficiency and arrogance had ruled over much—were here humble suppliants, eager to learn first lessons in spiritual laws, the manifestations of which everywhere are love, harmony, and justice. A former ruler over more than ten cities was here, beside him, who in ignorance and criminal contagion had never known or had never availed himself of opportunities to understand any of the beatitudes of life.

I had then and there an opportunity to draw some simple deductions, which, for the reader's benefit, I will state in three conclusions, namely:—

1. That which you cannot take with you to the new life is not worth the struggle that men make to obtain.

2. That which ennobles and unfolds spiritual beauty is worth many thousand fold more than has ever been realized.

3. The consciousness of and obedience to truth, as spiritually perceived, constitutes the principal good, preparing the only states of spiritual happiness here and hereafter.

It was with mingled feelings of pity and gratitude that I now formed judgment, based upon actual facts, as I witnessed them in this sphere of spiritual existence: pity that there should be those for whose instruction institutious of the sort referred to were necessary,—that the voice of the conscious self had not been heeded in previous states, where experiences now seemed to me to have been as schools specially designed for primary teaching and unfoldment,—that, in humiliation and shame, expiation had become necessary for advancement in the life of spirit.

This was the dark side of the great object lessons which were shown to me.

There was undoubtedly much value in the exhibition and its inductions.

I also saw here some illuminated intelligences, whose rank and the purpose of their being present I did not understand; but in a short time was made aware that their presence was not a meaningless display,—that there was a reverse side of the picture,—that while for many the broad road so graphically described in scripture was essentially and correctly stated, there were also others whose attractions separated them from the multitude,—those attuned to finer vibrations—whose ears were open to spiritual harmonies,—to whom, up to that moment, prevailing conditions had been discordant. Unable to respond to the current of passing events, they had remained merely interested spectators, observing the situation,—yet wholly apart and unconcerned.

Personally, I believed that similar general laws prevailed here as in the sphere of my former life, and that other laws would be revealed in due season. I felt that if, in the providence of the universe, the sparrow was protected, I should not be left in ignorance, without opportunities to learn the compass of Deity.

Soon the offices of the illuminated intelligences were made known. The needful ones received many evidences of love and wisdom, through vibrations and other methods of communication, exquisite harmonies, of which no one spoke or sought an explanation, for to each were conveyed impressions distinctly different from those received by others, yet all perfectly adapted to special needs, leading or seemingly attracting them in different directions.

Let it not be inferred, when I speak of a spirit's going in another direction, that actual necessity is laid upon any one to travel in the earth sense. It is true that some spirits can, by their own volition, pass immense distances, and, in so doing, practically annihilate space. Such travelling through stellar spaces of the universe are constant occurrences,—not, however, to escape the contagions of vice or lower companionship, for only those who have realized spiritual growth possess such power.

All unfoldments are, in their nature, esoteric and not limited by time or space. They are rather evolutions from lower to higher realizations of spiritual thought, and each sphere in the upward life, when fully attained, permits the spirit to enter into harmonial relations with those with whom it is in natural uniform correspondence.

The power of spirit transference, or capacity to pass through space by will alone, will explain, upon planes of lower habitation, the presence of those whom many would naturally expect to find only after eons of progression, in higher and divinest states.

At this time, it was signified to me that enlarged opportunities for spiritual study and observation were obtainable by conformity to conditions required of all, and that I could enjoy such opportunities as my previous life had prepared me to receive and comprehend. There were placed, subject to my selection, many courses of procedure in which lessons were to be learned, leading to fuller and clearer consciousness of the beautiful and perfect law of spirit.

I now saw that it was not impossible to pass from planes to mountain heights, and that powers of vision and conceptions of sacred harmonies surrounding me were in exact relation to my spiritual perception and capacity of receptivity, now being more perfectly unfolded through new experiences.

I also saw that labors brought no fatigue. My eyes, heretofore unaccustomed to such brilliancy of light, acquired larger capacity to relate to all changes of conditions.

Upon the journey, which I now entered, I passed through different altitudes, in all of which there seemed to be so many kaleidoscopic changes that at first I could not fully comprehend my surroundings. My robe changed its texture, and in each transformation I received new, poetical, and harmonial suggestions of eternal love and wisdom, each more entrancing than the other, in-breathed, absorbed, and assimilated through atmospheric and spiritual influences, leading me away from the low and groveling conditions in which I had but recently seen so many, out into glorious light and liberty of the divine being, infinitely superior to the limitations of material states.

From certain altitudes I beheld, at great distances, cities and villages, with their multitudes of busy and conglomerate populations,—many architectural curiosities, crystal streams, flowing from mountain peaks, rearing their lofty heads into space, from which wave vibrations were received, each one signifying to me the spiritual and intellectual fact, that I should and could pass into closer relations with the great masters and adepts, upon whom wondrous powers over elements had been conferred.

The vibrations, which I then began to study, conveyed interior meanings to all who had learned to wisely translate them. By them an universal language could be understood throughout immeasurable space.

I learned that all languages are but gross reflections of thought vibrations, having their origin in spirit, but that environments and conditions have had much influence in their technical expression and evolution. I perceived that man living in lower spheres, under material influences, has not yet aquired ability to sense a higher and universal harmony, and that at most, after years of practical effort, he can gain mastery of but very few rates of vibrations, bringing him into correspondence with perhaps one, two or three languages,

What more beautiful and positive evidence of his origin and final destiny than the capacity and desire for control over a greater number of vibratory sounds, as illustrated in lingual acquirements?

Every word, every thought sent forth as evangels of good or as destructive vehicles of evil, find their counterparts in expression. Emanating under inspirations of love and harmony, they reach the heights, and add to the sum of heavenly effluences, preparing new conditions and better inspirations for those who have overcome, substituting, in the heart, light for darkness and so unfolding divinity.

And while I reflected upon what had been revealed by the new experiences, it seemed to me that men upon earth should, through revelations of spiritual light, be able to unfold similar and allied states of being,—that an universal religion, developed through sensitiveness to etheric vibrations and a realization of the divine in consciousness, would soon, enable the world to evolve spheres of more perfect harmony, and that thereby humanity could hold sweeter and closer relations in all states of existence.

It was but a short time, however, before I was awakened from that state of meditation and made to feel that for me, at least, in the path I had selected to follow, there were great labors, services to render, for the due performance of which in the court of conscience, I should be required to answer.

I learned that the ability to translate facts into esoteric meanings had not been conferred for useless purposes. That in the condition of spirit life there existed the law of service and obedience, to both of which I owed special obligations which, even had I so desired, could not have been evaded or transferred to others.

I now understood the objective purpose of my visit to those strange and, to me, new spheres.

Floating in the atmospheres, I perceived individualized thoughts, desires, prayers for spiritual assistance, relief from suffering, and thousands of seeming misfortunes. I was taught to discern through aural colorings the peculiarities of each separate entity, with which my greater sensitiveness now brought me into close relation. I clearly perceived my mission; the duties pertaining to my chosen occupation were clearly revealed. I had, in fact, become a laborer in spiritual realms of the Infinite, a messenger of hope and light.

Upon earth I had striven, largely through book and pen, to instruct and lead others; now I recognized the necessity and desirability of another form of service,—that in love and sacrifice for others one only could attain the absolute good.

While in earthly states one may at times feel encouraged in all humanitarian efforts, there are also periods of mental and spiritual depression arising from causes needless to refer to now.

Not so is it, however, in the life of spirit.

For wise and, as I now understood, beneficent reasons, time had been completely eliminated from calculations. Accomplished purposes fix and mark the boundaries and limitations of individual expressions. Hope, born of former successes and harbinger of yet greater victories, sustains and encourages the spirit in all labors of love, thus redeeming the promises of old.

I could here sit in the councils of the great and wise, learn new things, and receive inspirations of all the ages.

Slowly, through evolutions of conscious harmony, the beatitudes of the heavenly states of existence inspired to renewed efforts, so that instead of sharing only, I should become, through mastery of conditions, the creator and dispenser of celestial manna.

Who were these great and noble ones?

They had come up out of great tribulations; had wrought in the heat of day, borne heavy burdens, and now rejoiced, not in complete victory, for they were yet workers in the vineyard, doing and hoping much, and through results of noble personal experiences, were encouraging others to continue, and resign not farther efforts for the attainment of those spiritual gifts which always enable the possessing ones to do much for humanity, and the unfoldment of the divine self.

I have spoken of the visible thought, forms, and aural colorings of their surroundings. Millions upon millions of such manifestations, each a symbol of the aspiration of the human heart,—not manifest to us, sometimes hardly visible as separate entities,—yet easily perceived by those in correspondence,—exist in the pure ethers.

A spirit soon learns how to group and separate the forms created through various thought vibrations, to analyze and estimate their importance, and to reject, as worthless, even harmful, petitions, quantities of them constantly visible, literal answers to which would be either impossible, or, if permitted, would prove a worse visitation than the penalties which the petitioner may have been expiating, and thus seeking to escape.

It is a truth, very apparent in spirit conditions, that mortals (here I refer to immortals in relations to the mortal body) have but very imperfect conceptions of their own greater needs.

We hope, however, as better means of intercommunication are established through gifted and delicate persons, to be able more fully to explain the interrelations between the two spheres of activities, and the laws governing each. To this end, new and specially prepared instruments are being constantly used by the spirit world, and we feel that our labors, through them, will result in better conceptions of truth.

We never weary in our efforts, for we well know that as we succeed in lifting the standard of moral and ideal life, so also shall we create more harmonious conditions, an ample answer back, to all our sacrifices and struggles.

There is a general, and if I may use the word, an average or universal moral atmosphere or expression, separate and distinct from individualized personality. To that general or modern civilization, in its relations to moral states, we turn, for it represents to us the realized sum total of human wisdom, love, harmony.

In our communications, we are obliged to overcome general as well as special conditions, in order to assist individual cases.

Therefore, you will perceive that all obligations of citizenship are important, maintaining or lowering the average, according to the thought and the action.

In the sphere or state to which I have alluded, I saw many intelligences who, like myself, for the time being, had formed no clear conception of the ultimate and perfect condition. They, at least, seemed to be satisfied with their present beautiful surroundings; for myself, I could not say so much.

The prevailing conditions, and acceptance thereof as entirely satisfactory by these intelligences, caused me no little anxiety and considerable speculation.

Here were students from all schools of philosophy, astronomers, scientists, and vast numbers from other intellectual conditions of earth. Some of them had been here centuries, reckoned in terms of years, and, from all I could see or learn, they were perfectly content, not seeking or expecting change. They regarded not the principle of natural attraction; and, practically rejecting the teachings of evolution, condemned them as quite impossible, and unworthy investigation of the thoughtful and the wise.

Why and how could such a condition or state of mind continue so long? Why had not a greater light and a higher wisdom been revealed to those satisfied ones?

To answer such natural inquiry, it will be necessary to review, in a few words, some earth history of one or two of my personal acquaintances whom I found there.

In the earth they were called "scientists "; and, as sciences were then known, they were almost wholly occupied in the discovery of the laws of physics or chemistry, for instance,—learning much and teaching much concerning the hidden facts in nature. Theirs were exoteric approaches toward The Light; but, unfortunately, their own magnetic, positive and objective attitudes constantly obscured and prevented them from perceiving that which might have led them out of material into clear and pure spiritual conceptions. Desires for discoveries of facts were not wanting; methods only failed. They built their houses upon the plains and in the valleys.

Those pure and earnest truth seekers, upon wholly material lines, failed to discover the Divine Ego,—the pure gem, constantly emitting its bright, steady, flawless rays of absolute white light. They were not sinners above others. They performed good and necessary work.

Is it not assigned to man to find out God?

Where can He be found except as manifested in His laws?

They simply misconstrued the evidence of their own discoveries, and sought to relegate spirit and exalt matter, substituting shadow for substance. Some of them are yet so engaged, and thus far the higher expressions in matter only have been revealed to them. Are they not living examples of the principle of correspondence? They will eventually apply their great learning and keen powers of penetration and analysis to the study of spiritual laws, and naturally, slowly, possibly imperceptibly to themselves, will grow to higher states, surpassing present limitations, practically illustrating the evolution of the lower consciousness into the image of the higher.

Instead of endeavoring to find correspondences existing between spirit and matter, as conditioned through the manifestations of spiritual forces in all spheres or lives, thereby discovering true indices of progress and possibilities of future unfoldments, they sought to exalt outward substances only,—the vehicle of the real,—following will-o'-the-wisps, evading the main issues of life, the positive purpose of existence, controverting principle, substituting nothing, and are now substantial confirmations of what I long ago perceived,—that sometimes what the world esteems an education, instead of becoming the pinions upon which the spirit may mount to infinitely exalted heights, it often proves to be manacles and weights, enslaving the soul until every darkened cell of the mind has been permeated by celestial light.

As in physical and lower states of mental action, so in higher conditions of moral and intellectual life, the fixed, eternal law of conscience and personal responsibility—without atonement or evasion through any one or by any means—holds each and every child of the universe to its unalterable purpose. Every true path is straight; wanderers there-from must retrace their steps. The dim light of a dark lantern often leads astray, but the glorious light of the eternal sun brightens and simplifies every course.

It now seemed that I had gained all desirable benefits, all obtainable light and experience from surrounding conditions, and that my first effort should be made in behalf of others, in special activities which I had elected.

Like all neophytes, beholding a world, largely in the depths of moral darkness, my zeal knew no bounds. It appeared at first as though single handed I could lift the whole inert mass, permitting light to penetrate every nook and corner, turning millions from darkness to better and clearer conceptions of truth.

I had not learned much concerning the relation of objective and subjective forces of the universe, and that one force was the antithesis of the other, and so expressed in universal law for wise, beneficent, specific purposes,—that upon the subjective side of life there were limitations to spiritual powers and control,—that zeal without wisdom often proved profitless indiscretion,—in fact, that I must learn by hard and bitter experience how to apply my newly acquired powers, in order that the last state of man should not be worse than the first

In different conditions of spirit life, some are taught, some led in chosen occupations, working out their own salvation, redemption, progression, becoming their own church redeemer, teacher, for it is the law that he that giveth is, in fact, he that receiveth; he that doeth much suffereth naught; the world puts its richest gifts at his command, and heaven itself adopts him.

Perceiving and understanding the law, is not the call to every one to accept it? Does light shine into darkness to increase that darkness?

There are, in the spirit world, opportunities for reflection, for philosophical deductions, for self-examination, and for the application of spiritual teachings; also a certain liberty of action,—a full measure of judgment, a review of evidential probabilities from what has preceded, pictures of possible attainments, but each one marks his own trail and methods of procedure. History repeats not. Like causes produce the same results, but expressions of causes come to each in perceiving aural colors, and upon different planes,—to the neophyte, confusion, to the illuminated, absolute order and unity. The measure of comprehension is evidence of celestial illumination. The light is all about, permeating infinitude. It may be night to some, noon-day brightness to others. Darkness is heavy and holds to earth. Light has a double meaning. Its children can explore the Pleiades and lay their trophies at the feet of aspiring students.

Having now entered upon the new occupation of spirit, if I may so term it, I became intensely interested and anxious about results, so much so that I frequently failed in final accomplishments. I could not come into rapport with organisms that I desired to influence, nor could I control other conditions to my liking. " The Prince of the Power of the Air," of which I received intimations, and had previously read—a power intangible and be-yond vision, at least of those in my state, yet veritable and perhaps the stronger force of the universe—holds in check the enthusiasm and misguided zeal of those under the dominating influence of the heart, uncontrolled by wisdom. Here, as upon the mortal plane of spiritual manifestation, there must needs be long preparations before the regal crown of authority sits upon the brow of experience. Individuals and personalities count for nothing. What matters a tiny spark when the world is afire? Was I not once a citizen of the small and insignificant planet called earth? Are there not in-numerable billions of souls thronging the courts of infinite space, who have not yet even learned if there be such a home, prolific of life and immortal hopes? Are my little efforts for the good of a few old acquaintances, neighbors, and citizens important factors? How much and how long shall the spirit hope and labor? Come down from Parnassus and build a simple and plain hut out of the woof and warp of common things. You must learn the use of practical tools and instruments in constructing your new home. Heretofore, in fancy, you have been living with the gods. Now you must bear heavy burdens along dusty roads and earn the mendicant's scanty meal,—that humility, patience, obedience, and the law of sacrifice for others shall bear fruit, opening the doors to more beautiful visions, and leading into serener atmospheres, where more of love and wisdom, more of God shall be revealed through your own interior correspondences with new and better things. You must learn the power of concentration, that at your command the spiritual forces of the universe shall work for practical results. Instead of governing a world, as in your enthusiasm seemed possible, learn the real value of a single soul, and start that aright in fulfillment of ultimate destiny. So, anticipating time, supplementing the experience of your brother with the larger experience of your own, he may also receive some light, and upon it build mighty aspirations and hopes, the fruition of which shall satisfy his longing spirit.

So, seeking to incorporate the philosophy of spirit into tangible, veritable issues, one learns and unlearns the earth lessons of all the ages. Sometimes he retraces the paths so laboriously marked and travelled in the dark night of experience, hope almost gone, finally reaching the sunlit course, now so straight, plain, that the simplest child of nature need not err therein.

Wherefore and for what are all these things in the loom of nature? Not by chance, nor by inert, sluggish inactivity, does the spirit come to harmony with the Great Oversoul. Disorder and apparent discord are all your own, fortunately finite, perishable. From the heights you will view your present surroundings,—the picture will be beautiful, harmonious in every detail,—truth constituting the perspective, all its colorings, love.

So, with intimations of a successful outcome, inspired and to be made a fact through knowledge of natural law, I now go forth into larger missionary fields of the world. When a mortal, sensitive to such vibrations as I command can be found, then to express through that one in written hieroglyphics some unknown facts of life, a knowledge of which shall encourage weary ones to renewed efforts, loftier aspirations, and better hopes.

So, from the genesis of aspiration, may ultimately evolve great souls, and rejected stones become luminous, adorning the inner chancel of consciousness.

The heart of man, always desiring something better while upon the plane of mortal habitation, never ceases its higher, nobler aspirations for larger liberty and better satisfactions.

As it aspires there, so here. Does it love in mortal states?—far more truly and intensely here.

We but enter new schools, where atmospheres are clearer, vibrations quicker, love more intense, playing upon organisms keenly sensitive to delicate forces of spirit, passing through refined and subtle ethers over spaces inconceivably vast, each selecting its mate, prepared for it before history's remotest ancestor had learned to utter his first guttural sounds, harbingers of ultimate evangelization of the world.

Thus prepared, the spirit, clothed in a garb neither subject to heat, cold, nor disease, knowing no darkness, impelled at first by loving remembrances, after that by a greater love,—beholding the necessities of all, possessing capacities coextensive with the human needs, requiring only evolution in methods of applied usefulness, goes forth upon its missions of love. Thus every success of spirit, increasing hope in the heart of mortality, also enlarges the horizon of spiritual perceptions. What may await its first efforts, I hope more fully to explain in other chapters.

CHAPTER II.

Having thus far, and in the manner described in the previous chapter, prepared myself for the exercise of delicate and useful functions of spirit, why should I not make the attempt at influencing the spirit in mortal form? Should I not go to those whose disposition, habits of thought, and predilections were understood? This is what natural inclination would dictate, and, in fact, what usually occurs, though there are cosmic souls who seem equally at home anywhere. Not so, however, in the special case under consideration. I felt that some vibrations, charged with electrical and magnetic force, sent forth through impulsions of love, even if bearing evidence to the recipient, of being the frail efforts of a neophyte, might bear some fruit under friendly conditions,—more certainly, in-deed, than if subjected to the cold, austere analysis of those who, possessed of prejudices, forestalled any suitable conditions for spiritual influx.

I leave the reader to infer, after this statement, where I directed my first efforts. It is not my purpose to deal in personalities or to make names public, some of them well known, and a few yet among you; some, however, have passed to this side of life. Suffice it to say that many investigations and lectures have from that time been the result of my mission, some of them by professors who have discovered great things and announced so much as has seemed desirable for present good.

The work has only commenced, but I am gratified with achievements already made and hope to aid, by my suggestion and inspiration, in yet more important discoveries and revelations which will be for the benefit of coming ages.

To some readers, time may seem of great importance, that the work lags, and that the clouds of ignorance, prejudice and superstition gather with increasing force, and so present insurmountable walls, moats, defences.

Do not fear. Is it not recorded that a pebble slung from the right arm of youth slew the chosen giant of the enemy? So shall it ever be.

When it became evident that one gifted son of earth had perceived the deeper meanings of life (which I helped him to realize), and had begun to seek and know more of truth, I felt that I had not served without purpose and that the importance of rejected facts in his life which I had been seeking to impress upon him had indeed in him become the keystone in the temple, the foundation of which was at last laid deep in his soul, secure and safe from attacks of ignorance and bigotry.

In the hierarchy of spirit, that court of review, if I may be permitted so to call it, in order to convey to human intelligence some idea of spiritual order and accountability, the deeds and actual achievements of every human soul are properly weighed and estimated. Here, divested of all personal considerations, without prejudice, without favor or praise, all that has been achieved or is worthy of consideration receives its reward; but no deed or series of successful labors does in any manner absolve the soul from further efforts. The spirit thereby is only strengthened and encouraged to go forth, having received recognition of its usefulness and capacity for possible higher, better, nobler achievements. Revelations of future possibilities come to the willing aspirant upon planes of present habitation, and it is for each to embrace and to make effective the immediate work lying before him. He must, and will soon, learn that order is indeed one of heaven's first laws, and that delegated duties bear strict relation to spiritual hopes, desires and capacities. One service in no way relieves from responsibility ; other services command, which open more beautiful and diviner perspectives of life, with serious, deep import to the aspiring, yearning spirit; for as powers are unfolded, corresponding and relative responsibilities follow, and thus greater hopes, expectations and desires constantly press for satisfaction.

Is not the spirit on its way toward perfection? Shall it not find correspondences in subtler manifestation and deeper realization? Truth is round, not angular, reflecting beauty and radiations from all points of its circumference, every view evolving new realizations of being, new glories, new attributes, inciting aspirations for more truth,—the sum of all which, in itself, being the very essence of Divinity.

While my spirit was thus reflecting upon its own inherent powers and possibilities, judgment was pronounced, through the involution, absorption, harmony, created by the very deeds which I unwisely supposed would be the subject-matter of special consideration of those in superior states of unfoldment.

I learned by this first practical proof, which was so impressed as to become indelible, that I should henceforth live in atmospheres of my own creation,—that achievements of spirit created states of being, corresponding precisely with the importance of duties performed; that my supposed judges, constituting the hierarchal court, were but vice-gerents, executing the law's decrees; and that harmonial relations to law, through obedience and worthy deeds, could be outworked, leading one into aural surroundings where he could understand methods of reward and experience divine satisfactions.

This was my first effort. I perceived its lesson, its recompense in consciousness. I had learned a principle, a law, and had practically come to a knowledge of its personal application. One step forward! Revelations were now sensed as the answer of service, a many-fold equivalent, a perpetual incentive, divorced from all selfish desires for special benefits, leading to the heights.

But, while I could thus for the moment reflect and look into an imaginative future, hoping and expecting much, I was reminded that no victory which came unsought, without struggle and confident trust, was ever inscribed upon any banner,—that I was now entering the corridors of celestial experiences, faintly catching the first glimmerings of light, and was not able to behold the full brightness of the heavenly galaxy reserved for those who had labored and achieved.

All these gentle reminders, coming from hearts of love and wisdom, soon led me to more fully consider the results of my efforts, and to institute comparisons between my own and their state of illumination, and the reasons therefor.

Having thus discovered that there was no quick or immediate means by which spirit could pass from lower to highest conditions of conscious power, that others—exercising control over elements, executing laws, and possessing many gifts at present not at my command—had been denizens of earth, living in remote periods, surrounded by no special advantages which had not been conferred upon myself, then came unto my own spirit a conviction, a settled determination, that I also must begin in renewed energy of purpose to unfold individual, inherent, dormant capacities of spirit, and that to the end of perfecting those resolutions, every opportunity for diviner unfoldment should be utilized.

Up to that moment I had principally relied upon myself, aided only by such intelligent assistance as had been either voluntarily given or attracted to me under laws not fully understood. I had not escaped the karma of earth. I still relied upon the sufficiency of those experiences and intuitions developed in that form of being. It may be a fact that even in those conditions I had partially conceived the importance of spiritual aid, had, according to the light of lower vibrations, sought harmony, and not without answers that then appeared to satisfy the longings of my heart.

Here, however, I was confronted by new aspects of the eternal law, operating in states to which I had but recently attained, to the full import of which I was a seeming stranger. I remembered that formerly, when in doubt, I sought the construction of law from constituted authorities. Why should I not apply to the wise for information? Could I not thus supplement my limited experiences?

Understanding some of the differences existing between the two states,—that upon earth enacted law is prohibitive, all things being legally permissible, not restricted or wholly denied, while spiritual laws are positive, commanding, exacting strictest obedience in every detail, and to him that through faithful compliance overcomes, conferring blessings beyond conception,—why should I not sit at the feet of wisdom, and learn from the vice-gerents of the Great Oversoul, whose radiations permeate every part of an infinite universe, in whose effluences these, my desired teachers, had become partakers of that whereof I had not attained?

Such were resultants of perceived limitations,—leadings of spirit upward, seeking harmonial relations with those whose light was sufficient unto my present needs.

"I will arise and go unto my Father's house." If my robe of deeds will not admit to the guest table, I will be as an hired servant.

Some time, I know not when, it may be that I shall be accounted worthy of a higher place—but there, at least, I may learn, if not directly, then through others, some beautiful, instructive lessons, which shall lead me out of my present encompassed, impeded, self-imposed restrictions, into acknowledged equality with those from whom now, in humility, I must seek instructions, that I may attain spiritual preferments, powers, and larger possibilities of service.

Why should I not, through the infinite ethers of space, send forth electrical forces charged with wondrous psychic powers, sufficient to influence the most obdurate? Such aspirations mark the genesis of new unfoldments. Here the lower had unconsciously been paying homage to the higher self.

Unawares, I had been sitting at the feet of a Gamaliel and seizing upon so much wisdom, beauty, truth, as corresponding unfoldments permitted me to receive, although for the time I did not understand Divine methods of teaching. Nor did I see the path clearly marked leading to victory.

As so many upon your plane, so here, multitudes whom no man can number, have not learned that the chief battle, and the principal foe to be fought and overcome is within, or rather outward environments and the karmas' created thereby, prevent divine expression from within in perfect relations to truth.

The ministry of ignorance often serves for the unbuilding of worlds, holding its victims to the conditions of material labors, thereby creating surroundings making possible a physical life necessary for great teachers, who have from time to time blessed mankind by their presence,

Shall I not come into companionship with my own? From of old, was I not one with them?

Has a few short years' absence upon earth, for special expiatory purposes, forever excluded me from those I loved?

I will appeal to the God within. Before His throne, established in my own consciousness, I will plead the cause with all the eloquence, pathos and love that I can command, and ask that the path of duty be made plain, and that, emerging from darkness to light, wisdom shall teach and lead. By virtue of my divine inheritance and possessions, I shall receive that which I ask. I will not grovel in the dust. I will walk, demanding that which I know the Infinite never denies,—that I should no longer be subjected to powers whose authority I oppose and contradict, whose temporary reign, in my night of humiliation and darkness, I now spurn and reject.

While thus standing, disputing the authority of an imaginary foe, an unreal entity, I beheld, at first in the dim distance, a bright, beautiful star, shining in all the lustre of perfect brilliancy and splendor. It seemed to be far away, infinitely distant, but I could perceive its atmosphere. The vibrations from it were charged with divine elixirs: peace, harmony, love and triumphant joy were all blended in its aural colorings. There came to my spirit indescribable and heavenly satisfactions, bidding, urging me to leave behind the heavy burdens of sin, and evermore to keep in view its perfect light, which would never disappoint nor desert; and that, in the upward journey, amid all the trials and conflicts, struggles, apparent defeats and positive victories, never to lose sight of or forget, even if temporarily obscured, the permanent existence of that which had been revealed unto me for guidance and inspiration.

Through an esoteric unfoldment, preparing one for deeper progress in the life of spirit, I had, by this object lesson, been consciously brought into close relations, new to me, possibly, and in so far as my experiences extended, peculiarly personal. The immediate lessons, or teachings, had been to direct my notice to a distant, bright and uplifted object, upon which I had been told to fix my attention, keep it ever in view and, if under trying circumstances I should be tempted to depart from the course marked, never to forget its existence. There was the beacon, signifying to my spirit, hope, perpetual, watchful care, by its constant presence. An object, fixed in the distance, capable of emitting rays of special brightness, peculiarly attractive, then seemed to me the highest reward in spiritual attainments. I had not learned that this light was subject to many apparent changes in appearances. It had not been revealed that its aural colorings would quickly respond to my own thoughts, aspirations, hopes and deeds. It seemed afar off, but something which the spirit would long to reach, and under the influence of which one could enjoy the sunshine of an eternal life of bliss.

Poor, inexperienced, unsatisfied child, in a universe of spiritual forces, conditions, hopes, the laws of which you know not, and the means, methods of study, objects of attainment unrevealed, unlearned.

How could I know the mystery of mysteries? I will take my journey to that distant orb, explore its wonders, and make my abode there,—possibly in some quiet and selected nook or dell, a new, permanent home, better furnished and equipped for the service of spirit. It may be there, in sweet companionships and highest spiritual communions among those who have overcome all things, through love, I will learn how by leaps and bounds to reach the heights and see my God and His Christ face to face. Therein the hopes and longings of my spirit had until now been denied. None of my sweet, loving, and wise friends had ever beheld the face of the Father. Wherein they had failed, I must succeed. Had I not been so taught? Is it not true? Some vibrations of spirit seem to answer back, yes and no. I could not divine the meaning of those distinct and positive impressions. Yes, there is a Father and His Christ. Of this fact you have been taught aright. Did not my friend, the poet, say, " I hope to see my Pilot face to face "? Well, I know poets sometimes write with considerable beauty. Do they always express the real, absolute essence of facts? What does he think upon this great subject now? He must have been right, for indeed he was inspired.

While thus reflecting upon some of the conditions of life in spirit, I was suddenly awakened to another more material, but necessary fact. In the outset of my spiritual awakening, had I not selected a vocation? Had I not chosen to become a messenger of light and truth? Was not my theatre of labors to be upon earth and among those whom I had but recently known?

Instead of seeking the face of my Pilot, whom those many centuries in advance of myself had never beheld, why not labor faithfully in my chosen pursuit? Could I not in this manner fix foundations upon which to erect a better superstructure? Could one vibrating upon planes of my present habitation behold face to face the supernal light of Deity? Go back to earth, labor according to the light of your knowledge, seek greater wisdom, and learn more perfectly how to fulfil present duties. Possibly there, in the due performance of assumed obligations, you may some day behold reflections of the Father and learn more about the spirit of the Christ.

And while I was, in this manner, shown the path of duty, the beacon light seemed nearer, shining with special brilliancy. Is there a relation between it and His Christ? Time and experience will surely reveal the truth. If I may not now go to that distant orb, will not the light come to me? It had already come as near as my conditional existence, under the law, the operation of which I did not understand, would for the time permit.

I think I have already referred to the law of attraction or the assimilation of similars. That law is very far-reaching in its operations,—through it one may become allied in thought, and finally in companionships with the great, illuminated ones, possessing powers beyond mortal conceptions, and controlling elemental forces in infinite space.

In states of ignorance, rejecting opportunities, and seeking only conditions, the antithesis of truth and harmony, one also experiences the binding chains of sin, in its myriad hideous forms of expression, and thus is held for ages,—until expiation and restitution are made for all things.

The eternality of law and its absolute control in all affairs of earth and heaven, fixes the present state of every child in the universe. He can, however, develop sufficient powers to change his spiritual relations to the law,, if he so wills.

What, then, should be the chief duty and purpose in life? My reply is, " Study spiritual laws all emanating from Infinity" and learn their operations and results; seek to fulfil those conditions through which harmony may evolve in all relations where and howsoever the spirit may be outworking its final destiny.

Karma is but a term, rather indefinitely defining man's relation to law, its outward definitions and expressions. It is, however, portrayed by means of aural colorings, which enable those in psychic correspondence and under clairvoyance to perceive one's present state of spiritual progress. It is, therefore, useful to study its conditions and varied manifestations.

Those who have attained powers sufficient thus to perceive and translate character are particularly fortunate, and can enter careers of special usefulness.

In my labors, now again taken up, I began to perceive my great needs and limited powers,—that I ought more thoroughly to perfect my own capacity of sight, and perceptions of others through laws of vibration.

Up to the present time I had given the study of laws, or their manifestations, only a general and casual consideration, upon similar lines as those pursued by most persons in both conditions of being. Now, however, I saw and felt, from practical experience, the special necessity of greater knowledge and a more complete philosophical understanding of the origin (if that was attainable), reason for and practical operation of all laws within the scope of my spiritual possibilities.

I had not then learned that all revelations of law come in correspondence with the necessities and unfoldments of spirit, under such conditions and at special periods of greatest needs,—that urgent requirements of spirit bring one into correspondence with vibrations, through harmonial relations with which every longing of the unsatisfied soul could be completely satisfied.

There came to me convictions of conscience; why had I not at the outset begun the study of spiritual laws under competent teachers? I had at first, in blind confidence, elected to become a messenger of light and truth. Had not the fate of blind leaders of the blind long since been declared? Could I hope to escape the penalties of my own folly, in electing to teach without due preparation?

Here at the very threshold of life under new conditions, a self-appointed leader and teacher of others had been confronted by conditions in regard to which his practical knowledge was indeed very limited.

Only one law,—how many others in the great laboratory of time and space had been evolved from Infinite Consciousness? Did I understand them all? Did I even know the origin or practical workings of even a single one of them? Stupendous ignorance! Go back to that primary school and take your place among those that knowing not, aspired not, and when thou hast received thy sight, then mayest thou walk alone, and in humility learn from willing teachers.

Now had I begun to realize the utter inadequacy of my preparations and partly to understand those required for successful labors in my chosen field.

I perceived that all spiritual powers bore certain relations to, and were expressed in personality, as upon earth, and that education, supplementing moral causality, was needful to success in all efforts.

I found that there were many whom I might desire to instruct, upon whom reason and other highest powers of spiritual knowledge must be brought to bear, if the mission I had at heart would prosper, enlarging the sphere of human knowledge, encompassing the world, the strong desire and chief hope of spirit.

The first ideals—born of enthusiasm, and recently acquired powers, of which I had not learned the limitations, inspiring me with the desire to accomplish all things, to forward to quick success the conversions of my old acquaintances, and enlisting their services, reach the State, nation, and finally evangelizing the world— began to give way. Other views succeeded, born of experience, in which high hopes and aspirations were doomed to determined resistance, if not absolute defeat. I perceived the causes of partial failures, for notwithstanding some had admitted bases and facts, others had wholly ignored them, and were actively denying the existence of a spiritual world, or any conditions whatsoever, of life, after physical death.

Herein I perceived a near correspondence between the two states of existence,— that in both, reason and arguments designed for conviction were used with similar liberties, and that neither state was free from errors.

There were in the life of spirit, under conditions in which I found myself, masses, innumerable hosts, more or less subject to the control of those who had achieved only a limited command over elements, and, I regret to say, whose conclusions were usually void of logic and reason, and frequently not worthy of respect, even.

I perceived that not only upon earth but in spirit, the fields of labor were beyond conceptions of boundary, and the harvest indeed infinite, laborers comparatively few, and I, a would-be-worker, a neophyte, unprepared, hardly knowing the instruments and methods, and wholly ignorant of their use. What would I do? Where begin? To whom apply? I will interrogate the star when its bright light once more shines unto my spirit. Where is it now? Was I not warned never to forget its presence? It had not of late been visible. It seemed eons of centuries since its light became dimmer; and in the interim I had been in the densest darkness, groping, wandering in ways I had not known. Had I constantly kept my eyes fixed in its direction, would not its light have led me aright? Shall I not invoke its return? Can I not evoke its presence from within my own consciousness? No longer will I leave my own soul tenantless! In all future efforts I will first seek the silence, and ask that the bright light once shown me shall again be my guide, leading me into all truth, by and through which I may yet attain to the heights.

Now I am no longer perplexed. I am beginning more clearly to perceive my duty and receive foregleams of the final outcome of my labors. I have been attempting to circumnavigate stormy and boundless seas without chart, rudder, or compass, all of which have been at my command, only concealed through the withdrawal of that Light, which would have been as a lantern unto my feet all along the way.

For the time, as I had allowed it to pass from consciousness, all the dark clouds of despair and hopeless discontent had settled around me like a karma, from which it seemed impossible to escape.

The first feelings of rapturous joy and triumph, imparted by confidence in the final outcome of the struggles in which I was then engaged, can never be expressed in words. I then felt and knew the real Father and His Christ, though both manifested their divine powers by other means than I had conceived.

It was not given me to behold either, face to face, as I had been taught to expect through some writings. Both had come unto my spirit as angel messengers, bearing messages upon planes of my own unfoldments, in vibrations which I could translate.

Did they speak to thee in audible tones? Spiritually, yes; materially, no. Did they announce their names or in any other manner indicate that they appeared in special personal forms? No.

Came they in the voice of the thunder, the loftiest peaks in heaven's own infinite space echoing back in monotones their glory, wisdom and power? No.

Did the Great Centre of Light show unto you His Throne of glory, toward which all are attracted? Did He invite you into His sublime, august presence? No, a thousand times, no.

Not by any such devious methods did I come to a realizing consciousness of that for which I had prayed and longed.

I had simply, by successful labors in the attainment of the good, in. humility opening my own heart to the reception of truth, placed myself in harmonial relations with one, or possibly more, of the beautiful, absolutely perfect and just laws,—the emanations of Infinite Wisdom. And, according to my progressive victories, had I realized the presence of the Author and His Christ.

And thus have they continued to speak and teach unto this hour.

Now, believing myself better equipped for the service of my fellow-beings, I saw that the field of labors had greatly enlarged, The scope and purpose of my new life had so vastly increased that all former horizons seemed to have receded into infinite distance. I could perceive the presence of want, of spiritual necessities in those accounted ignorant and lowly as well as among those who in pride of intellect had been inclined to reject such evidences as I had been able to present, with the special design of establishing through them the facts of existence beyond the veil of earth life.

In observing the results of my labors, I perceived that those whom in my previous life conditions I had accounted as useful and upright citizens in the walks of life, by some deemed humble, were less under the dominion of prejudice, more willing to receive truth and to profit thereby than were others from whom I had expected much.

Their environments, such as social influences, political and churchal aspirations, prevented not.

Many came within the influence of such vibrations as I was able to command, and were thereby instructed in regard to their correspondences therewith.

Some, in former lives, had been denizens in higher realms, and now, in unfortunate environments and lowly surroundings, were expiating for and correcting those defects of character that had held them in spiritual bondage, preventing converse and association in higher states of spiritual advancement. Among such I found willing, listening ears, gladly rejoicing, and trusting to join in celestial homes those from whom they had been long separated.

Not content with such ministrations as I could find occasions to render them, their spirits often came to me, while their heavily-burdened frames were seeking restorations in sleep. Marvellous spiritual experiences had been theirs, and instead of being a teacher only, I soon perceived that I was receiving new and clearer visions of truth, leading to higher, holier aspirations. Their weak vessels of clay were enclosing precious gems of wondrous beauty. In their spiritual homes, they soon learned truth, the law of life, and wisdom, becoming willing, obedient servants, in those understandings wherein services lead to honorable preferments and glorious issues.

Thus had the bright star of hope shown me a new and better way In walking therein I renewed and increased my spiritual powers, called to my aid those whom I knew not, came to circles where love reigned, drew around me those from many spheres who, as students and teachers, conferred much, insensibly, gently leading me into states of spiritual perception, where greater and innumerable victories became possible.

With each new purpose I was enabled to conceive methods that would achieve desired results. I began to sense higher, more beautiful vibrations in atmospheres charged with interior meanings, the existence of which I had not theretofore even suspected.

I felt that my spiritual powers had largely increased and that I was, relatively, perhaps, as important in my new state of being as in any relations I had before sustained to others in material conditions. I had obtained new glimpses, important to me, and in my imagination I pictured special positions of honor, great and highly unfolded intelligences as my companions. To what heights might not the spirit aspire? What metes and bounds could circumscribe its ambitions? Had I not escaped lower conditions at the outset of my celestial career? Did not the star lead to new revelations? Could not I now command its presence? I felt not quite so sure in that matter, I could not really assert that I had the power of its evocation at will. Previously it had been shown unto me after the fulfilment of duties and obligations. There were certain relations of spirit toward the law that seemed then to exact obedience. Possibly those are now conditions, compliance with which is required before desired blessing will be conferred. Such thoughts, passing through my mind, led me to reconsider, and to ask whether I might not have attempted independently that which I should have commenced in co-operation.

The light was indeed burning within, dimly, yet with sufficient radiance and power to compel a reconsideration of those ideas that I had but a few moments previously entertained. If I had become a child of light, a son of the bright star, why not strictly follow its teachings? Why should I attempt that in which I should probably fail? Was not evocation of higher intelligences and command of their wondrous powers reserved to those farther advanced in the heavenly way?

I was quietly bidden to review my first intentions,—told to strive for those victories within possibilities of achievement, that I had not yet reached the heights, that there were endless fields in progressive knowledge to explore.

For instance, had I learned the simplest elementary lessons in chemistry? Was not this a branch of knowledge which could be investigated in my present sphere of unfoldment? How could I go forward, leaving unlearned that which I might be required to know farther on? Without having acquired complete mastery in all details of every source of wisdom within my present surroundings, would I not be an unfaithful servant, unworthy to enjoy and possess the things reserved for use in future progressions?

Should I not faithfully labor, doing that which I could upon planes of present conception and understanding of duty without hope of reward?

Here was an opportunity to study the elementary principles of chemistry, that I might learn regarding those substances forming the body upon which I was dependent, under conditions by which I was then surrounded, and needful unto me in the performance of spiritual labors.

I was compelled to admit that I knew but very little about the subject. It seemed imperative that I should know much more. The laws of mathematics? Did I understand them? I had frequently met a distinguished professor in this branch of science. Instead of spending any part of my leisure opportunities in philosophizing upon subjects in regard to which I was not in correspondence to understanding^ receive all the truth, why not learn fundamental principles from those competent to teach?

Had I not, both upon earth and in spirit, neglected common, practical affairs, and without due preparation sought to dwell in empyreal atmospheres?

Then I began to realize that the foundations of absolute knowledge must be laid deep; that no superstructure, however symmetrical and beautiful its architectural design, was really secure unless founded upon the rock of absolute fact.

I had frequently read and, in a way, accepted the statement that all laws of the universe were based upon true mathematics. That, above all others, that was the one perfect science. How much had I really learned about the great truths involved therein?

I had spent an average life upon earth, really knowing and caring little about figures, which I now perceived were all the time representing eternal verities, exponents of perfect law.

Had I not entertained almost a total disregard for this whole subject? When in the material body I could never understand how certain friends should, from year to year, continue studying what appeared to me dry, hard, commonplace, mathematical, and geometrical figures conveying not much information.

Were these sciences what I then really supposed? Apparently not so to those who had delved beneath the surface and appearance of things. Those friends had been learning much concerning matters which I should not have neglected.

Unconsciously they were studying first principles, foundations of an infinite universe, whose maker and builder, called and worshipped under many names, is both Separate, Partless Unity, Absolute Wisdom. They were learning of and sharing that Wisdom, illustrated by those figures, much that you and I must know before we go forward.

I will seek my friends, and ask that in their class-rooms (for they are yet teachers) I, too, may be received as a pupil,—that I may come as a spirit in darkness, and be instructed in the rudiments of practical knowledge, so that having mastered basic principles, I may apply myself to the study of a more general knowledge included in mathematical summaries wherein I have found myself especially deficient.

About this period in my experience, I was constantly reminded by occurrences like in substance, if not in detail, to what I have here narrated, that the bonds of ignorance were still holding me to earth. I began to comprehend some of the facts of being,—that all the wisdom in each sphere of habitation must be thoroughly mastered in principle, and practically in methods of use and application, before I could hope to advance into other and higher conditions, and that before such unfoldment could be fully realized I should be subjected to thorough examinations, not only as to my progress in knowledge, but also required to give an account of my stewardship in the use and practical benefits conferred upon others through that which had been revealed to me.

Why had I in these directions delayed so long? Had I not been blind, not to understand how important and operative had ever been those wonderful laws about which I was now desirous of learning?

Only through knowledge of chemistry and mathematics could I hope to gain complete control over elemental conditions.

Without knowledge of the principles of these sciences I realized that I could not enter higher states of unfoldment; for is it not universal law that all things in correspondence must be assimilated before new revelations in consciousness are given? I perceived causes for my partial failure among those whom I had elected to serve.

Previously I had not been able to teach divine laws to those upon planes of higher intellectual unfoldments. I had been trying to approach them upon too material lines, causing antagonisms that naturally follow discussions of such subjects, between persons in earthly spheres. That I had not wholly divested myself of material conditions, was fully confirmed to me by the results of my efforts. Reason and argument emanating from other than truly spiritual sources are weak, proportionally ineffectual as they are suggested or evolved by material conditions.

Had I now attained to such light that I could again venture suggestions to certain ones? I was not wholly sure whether duty to self and those from whom I had received but little required that I should. Upon reflection I thought, however, to follow the leading of conviction, feeling that light would be given equal to every emergency and need. In pursuance of that conviction I went forth, special objects not fully defined, desires raised in aspirations for superior help. An angel of light preceded, pointing the way, directing my thoughts, delighting in my successes, and encouraging when my furled banner responded not to opportune breezes.

On this special mission what new lessons could I, out of my own limited knowledge, teach others? Was it not that one could, in all his struggles, appeal to those in superior states? That it was the law of life in heaven and earth?

I had myself neglected appeals to such sources, ignorantly supposing that I must independently work out my own destiny, not knowing the means for accomplishment of the purposes and ends of spiritual being. Was not it the essential position of those upon whom I was to impress and urge this great truth?

Would I be kindly received? As thoughts and difficulties of like nature were constantly obtruding, increasing the darkness, I was gently reminded to go forth in the service of spirit, working as the light was shown unto me, and told that rewards would be conferred by those who had attained to states of interior harmony, enabling them to justly correspond efforts and results.

I was advised that the seed-sower was not necessarily the harvester; that the harvester may not partake. Yet, from lowest to highest manifestation of laws throughout the universe, I consciously knew that there prevailed absolute harmony and perfect order, each particle of matter, permeated by spirit, evolving infinite designs through Nature's unerring laws, having their origin in sources where infinite wisdom, enthroned in supernal light, governs all things in perfect order, the original Cause, Source of every good. That which appears to mortals and all spirits in lower spheres other than perfect, is explainable upon the simple statement that such intelligences are not spiritualized and in harmonial relations to all truth, consequently are unable to perceive the perfect reign of order, truth and love, in what appears to them chaos, the rule of chance and fate.

I had been taught another and important lesson by these recent experiences, that of necessity for concentration and conservation of energy for specially selected fields of labor.

Heretofore I had been influenced by an inexpressible, indefinable hope, purpose, desire to aggregate all efforts, and immediately, by one supreme endeavor, accomplish that which seemed to me of such vast importance and appealing to higher consciousness.

In the light of subsequent experiences I now knew that such hopes were principally founded upon concentrated assumption and ignorance. The attendant spirit who had at first inspired my zeal, unfolded new conceptions of law, directed my labors in special channels, had departed from my conscious presence.

An important mission, however, for me had been shown. I had also received an object lesson not soon to fade from memory. Now that the light upon which I had begun to rely, under the intelligent rays of which I had assumed to walk in pride and strength of self-sufficiency, shone for me no longer, my spirit, heavily weighed, groaning under great perplexities, beset by trials, tribulations and anxieties not possible to name, or portray, would have sunken by the wayside and have sought relief through another life in a world of jarring discords like unto those I had so recently escaped, had I not at this moment caught the vibrations sent forth from one who had been an object of my recent ministrations. I perfectly translated those aspirations, longings, infinite hopes, dreadful doubts, ill-concealed fears, I perceived them from out the ethers of space, and knew to whom they appealed.

My night of despair vanished; the bright sunlight, with its glorious hopes, possibilities, radiated bliss, satisfaction, infused renewed zeal. An immortal soul had broken the shackles and chains which had so long bound and held it in subjection to material karmas. It had realized an emancipation, and the proclamation of truth had come through my instrumentality. Henceforth, let not my spirit be cast down,—the grovelling life and things of earth are naught to me,—spirit calls to spirit, and the deeper wisdom of heaven itself will surely in God's good time be fully revealed. I will hasten on the journey and some time come to the Mount of Transfiguration. There, laying aside all the garments which time and circumstance have woven around me, I will don a new robe, beautiful in texture, whiter than the driven snow; mine by right of conquest, an inheritance reserved through all the ages, in perfect harmony with love and the inner sources of all superlative radiations.

Gird on your armor again, raise it from the depths into which you have but just now cast it. It is already bright, and lighter and more attractive than when weary, footsore and distressed you sank under its heavy load. There are reserved for you new victories.

Go forth and teach some of the truths which you have been recently acquiring under your teachers. You will find great beauty, symmetry, order in that which before you could perceive but little, practically only means to ends,—that the adept therein might more readily exploit the necessities and ignorance of his neighbor.

You will find that both are intimate friends of the Great Architect,—trusted vicegerents, sent to harmonize apparent chaos, establish knowledge and the reign of law, teach conceptions of order, and through their mastery enable their obedient devotees to progress beyond others, becoming leaders, successful teachers, and with surpassing celerity, scaling seemingly impossible heights.

You will no more reject any form of spiritual expression, for you will understand better than before that every vibration in etheric space is freighted with knowledge from the Great Oversoul, and that as you aspire for all truth, so will you learn the law of its acquirement I raised my eyes to heaven, and, lo! the star was shining brightly.

CHAPTER III.

Through later experiences and from revelations, I perceived that the spirit could more perfectly comprehend the scope, order and purpose served by the life from which it had been released, and the reasons of penalties for disobedience of the law; that through its subjective memory it could recall the circumstances of each deed committed in the mortal state which, by reflection, became clearly visible, often reproduced as shadows of spirit, sometimes also shown as pictures, and for interpretation referred to the revelations of consciousness; that escape from undesirable visions was possible through aspiration and the life of spiritual supremacy, and that through such adaptation of means to ends one could pass into spheres, or zones, where even the reflection of evil does not obtain; that the visions of memory, though sometimes entailing the most intense forms of spiritual suffering, were indeed means under the cosmic law for the attainment of a more perfect unfoldment of all latent spiritual possessions.

It was also perceived that, in some respects, states of error corresponded to conditions taught by many upon earth as the purgatorial existence; that belief in the eternality of such relations should be rejected, though through the law of attractive correspondences its subjects were sometimes held in bondage for long periods; that the positive assertion of the spirit's prerogatives always unfolded clearer perceptions of reality and prepared conditions for entrance to more sublimated atmospheres and the subsequent enjoyment of greater freedom; that, through obedience to the law, the spirit in mortal life could acquire such sovereignty over the lower self that at will it could consciously inhabit spheres of thought where wisdom rules, and appropriate to its use and profit the effluences which there obtain, and that through aspiration a more perfect knowledge of the law could be realized; that the possessor of such light became a reflector of divine truth, inspiring others to seek the higher realizations of spirit, and that through a realization of the light one could become a teacher in the higher spheres of spiritual wisdom.

As upon earth, so in spirit he would have his admirers and followers, and would unconsciously receive a divine compensation in spheres of increased usefulness.

Such rewards became very beautiful object lessons to others seeking the truth.

The auras of those in the gloom of ignorance, as they obtained more wisdom, changed in color, and memory no longer recalled deeds and thoughts inharmonious to new and better ideals.

Aspiration, as a means of spiritual growth, could and should be employed by those seeking special guidance in every state of existence, and that through such methods the fields of usefulness and the horizon of spiritual vision could be greatly enlarged.

Divine realizations created a desire to obtain more light and to teach others the truth.

There were also other means susceptible of profitable employment, and that one could, in his first spiritual experiences and ever thereafter, derive signal benefits therefrom.

He might confidently hope to obtain abundant and satisfactory evidences of the spirit's final apotheosis.

Divine truth was revealed upon every plane where the spirit perceived, and the spirit in its progressive realizations was ever susceptible of wonderful unfoldment of its intuitive possibilities.

Thereby conditions were prepared for the influx of divine wisdom, and new states of being were evolved in deific correspondences.

Through every spiritual experience a higher consciousness could be unfolded and the spirit's latent powers more fully realized.

Concentration was the master-key unlocking many hidden treasures, confirming in the perfect light what hitherto had been but dimly perceived.

From the heights, the spirit could realize in constantly increasing and progressive ratios its relations to the Infinite Intelligence.

The intuitions of spirit distinctly revealed a probable final realization of absolute harmony.

Aspiration for the highest, accepting the evidences of truth, is always rewarded by a more perfect realization.

Hope became a mode of the spirit and served beneficent ends.

There were no ideal conditions of spirit perceived as visions in lower states of being, not possible to attain in the highest spheres; nor was the spirit limited to such ideations only.

Good thoughts, through the alchemy of spirit, were transmuted into cosmic forces and became agents for the individual realization of the Divine Unity.

Refined and purified thoughts became vehicles by means of which the illuminati taught the truth and pointed the way to absolute freedom.

The unchanging law led to the final centralization of spirit in the One Absolute.

The mortal conditions were repeated until the spirit fully apprehended and realized this central fact of being.

After many experiences, unperceived truth came as a revelation and enabled the spirit to realize its final destiny.

After having received new light, I perceived the necessity laid upon me of a more perfect idealization of the life. Hitherto, in the mists surrounding my varied experiences, though I had sought the pure light of truth, I had caught its scintillations and occasional rays but imperfectly. Experiences thus obtained had, however, served certain uses, but in my present state of being, reliance wholly upon them would have been like trusting to worn-out vehicles, no longer useful for the realization of cosmos.

Now I determined that henceforth I would seek to absorb the very essence of truth and love permeating infinite space, that I might scale the heights and behold the celestial light. Despite objective teachings and influences of earth, there is a spiritual light clearer than noonday sun, only obscured by clouds of my own creation. Nature, sublime and beautiful, has provided all the elements, and placed them at my disposal, when I shall have learned their spiritual meanings and made them subservient to loftiest aspirations.

Understanding the law and the possible attainment under it, I will further unfold my own divinity and lead others to seek wisdom from highest sources and appropriate all lessons that the truth inspires.

Should I not use my spiritual possessions for the glory of the Most High? Will not mortals upon earth listen to the new teaching? Yes, in a universal and general sense. No, or perhaps no, in the particular application. There are many souls desirous of light upon the general and abstract proposition, not, however, so amenable to special and personal methods of instruction.

Believing that spirit will respond to spirit, and that some one may be consciously led from chaos to order, from darkness to light, I will appeal unto the Highest for more wisdom and follow the light of divine intuition. I will again pass to earthly conditions, carrying with me new messages of truth and love. One friend has heard the call to search for the divine realities, others may also sense the vibrations of spirit and realize their meaning. Not science, art, poetry, music, nor any other attraction separately, but all combined in a divine harmony, will conspire to teach sacred lessons, and in them shall be found better than food, if neither meat nor drink, yet all-sufficient for the needs of humanity, which will sustain it in every condition of its existence, perpetually renewing aspirations, and preparing other and better conditions for, and in, the eternal now.

So, filled with spiritual light, I go forth in humbleness and hope, to teach the truth until it shall make those who come into its correspondence free indeed. I have now learned something of the limitations of spirit, and can wait upon infinite wisdom for results.

Having eternity at command, I do not fear the coming of the last hour, nor the sounding of any resurrection trump, calling me from the service of love. All calls to duty are, in a sense, new resurrections; all deeds performed in highest use, foregleams of other and better experiences. Hath it not been decreed that by the sweat of the brow, man shall earn his daily bread? Is not the law equally operative in all the infinities of space?

Having knowledge of the truth and that the ordinances of love are all synonymous and synchronous, I cannot fail in any sphere in which I may find attraction. The finer forces will always respond to every need of spirit, and become useful agents in unfoldment of its progressive destiny. The universe is man's, awaiting only his understanding of the condition for its possession. The omnipresent and unchanging law justifies the reason in all researches for its definition.

Great masters of the past have ever found wide fields in which to teach. So will it forever be in the future. As the horizon recedes, opportunities increase, and more interesting and beautiful panoramas delight the vision and urge me on. I have but to adapt myself to the law of conditions to become an inheritor of all wisdom which, though now but imperfectly perceived, is as old as time itself. The laws of the cosmos equally obtain in every sphere and condition of the spirit's existence, revealing to those in correspondence therewith beautiful syntheses. Such experiences inspire deepest reverence for the great source of all law and truth. With the realization of greater wisdom the spirit can teach more of truth, achieving victories where hope might well nigh have sought oblivion in eternal night,—were such a condition possible for spirit in any of its relations or conditions of being.

Now, better equipped, my spirit readily responds to the voice and the vision. Hope mounts upon pinions of love to celestial altitudes, and true altruistic ideals inspire my soul. The actualities of the spiritual life vary not in principle from the homely, necessary and useful duties of humanity. Are we not all included in the cosmic grandeur and in ratios as we serve the uses of spirit inheritors of the ineffable bliss? Yes, indeed. But here, also, the law speaks to us through its inexorable conditions, as unto the sons of earth. The soul that would obtain to the celestial harmonies cannot, except in obedience to the law, find the way of life, of truth, and infinite progression. For the law is the mode of the expression of the principle, the essence of being. Under its operation, all evolutions and harmonial relations obtain. The antithesis is chaos, loss of spiritual influence, dissipation of power, requiring rebirth, often through personal embodiments in states which, instead of commanding conditions, force the victims of such entailments to become servants unto those who have not acted so unwisely.

The will at the door of consciousness renders possible the attainment of a knowledge of the better way, in pursuance of which the lower karmic states can be avoided. The polarization of all spiritual aspirations in consciousness precedes illumination and the unfolding of the theocracy. This is the law of being. Let all understand the issue and be guided by its unchanging behest. Spiritual methods for obtaining supremacy in the hierarchies of heaven have been wisely left for intuitional discovery.

Through self-unfolded powers, each must outwork his own deliverance. According to his progression, he prepares conditions for the influx of divine wisdom. So is the progressive understanding of law revealed. Divine prescience is also more fully realized as one comes into harmonial relation with the law, and through it obtains to the mastery of the self. Finally, other and greater attainments (sometimes acquired only after centuries of struggle) endow the spirit with such wondrous powers that even a knowledge of them is wisely withheld from the neophyte.

Neither negation nor affirmation avail in the sphere of Divinity. There must be perfect unity and oneness before there is perfect realization of highest spiritual perception. There are, however, many calls of duty, many opportunities to teach in other and lower states or spheres where superior though not deific knowledge avails much. Through such associations, spirits incarnate and excarnate may enter into beautiful relations for mutual and useful purposes. Such associations are in accord with the law, though in the silence the apotheosis is more fully realized. There, as it were, the deep calls unto the deep, and the loftiest aspirations of the soul find spiritual counterparts. There, the perfect revelations are actualized in expression. There, also, all the deflected rays of light playing in the spiritual photospheres, in infinite varieties of expression and colors, so little understood, and which to many seem without purpose, are polarized in the pure white light. Through such experience the Omnipotent One, the Fountain of Law, is more clearly perceived in conscience and consciousness. Such are some of the lessons which have been given unto my spirit for divine uses.

Upon other occasions, I had not considered a knowledge of many spiritual conditions required for the conversion of others. Now, however, I perceived I could not go forth too well equipped. Antagonisms had been aroused through apparently very forcible arguments, against the teachings of the evidential phenomena, presented by my former friend and present co-worker.

It was desirable and necessary that I should reinforce his waning confidence, and also make more effective appeals to the consciousness of those inclined to accept the revealed facts concerning a future existence.

The everlasting cannot be understood nor realized through collateral evidences, The perfect law, in its entirety, is beyond human understanding and perception, but none the less self-existent and eternal. It is unconfined, and above time, space, or any other limitation. He that would gain an approximately clear perception of it must first evolve the divine self-consciousness. Such evolution must ever be an individual triumph; it places at the spirit's command the key which unlocks many secret occult avenues, all of which finally converge in the great spiritual highway, which needs not the sun, moon nor stars, for there infinite light is sufficient unto every traveller. Over those walking therein, angels keep watch; they are not permitted to go far astray. Through the understanding of divine methods, the followers of the light accomplish much.

Having obtained some light, I saw that the goal of the spirit's aspirations must be won, if at all, through appealing to the God within, through reason, intuition, spiritual perception, conscience and other divine attributes of the soul. Limitless the field for discovery. If the life and the aspirations of spirit upon the physical planes of existence find correspondences or counterparts in the spiritual, all the sweet harmonies in the infinities of space lead to success. Fear is eliminated, hope triumphs, and the light of consciousness shines in beautiful radiance.

What I subsequently observed and learned, all necessary prerequisites for the office of a messenger of light, will be referred to in the succeeding chapter.

CHAPTER IV.

s man's relations and attractions, realized through aspiration and the life, are the principal means through which he attains to higher states, and, as some are very sensitive to such correspondences, I naturally sought to reach those whose perceptions were unfolded upon planes similar to those with which I had been in harmonial relations when in the human form.

I felt that I could reveal to them important truths which had come to me concerning the spiritual existence, and which through them, could be used as valuable aids for the education of others, leading many to become living epistles, if you so please, of divine truth. I was desirous of more fully communicating many facts that I had been unable previously to reveal.

I felt that a knowledge of the law controlling the conditions of spirit life, if actually understood in its interoperations and influences, by even a single mortal, might ultimately, through that one, be transmitted to the race, and by its beneficent influence free many from the bondage of superstition, theological misconceptions and philosophical errors; that through such knowledge man would obtain a more complete mastery of his environments, be able to impart to others many facts concerning the superior state, regulate his own material occupations, select kinds of foods, and to ultimately establish better social and spiritual means of intercourse and education. It also appeared to me probable that other and possibly greater benefits than those here referred to would be received by interested disciples of those truths which I was seeking to teach, for I had learned that as a mortal spirit receives knowledge and attains highly important unfoldments, it realizes life and spiritual conditions in their cosmical relations, and not from the limited horizon of time and sense; that the spirit, as a condition of its own progress, must ever serve the needs of those in inferior states; that every son of the universe, by virtue of his spiritual possessions, however limited in expression, could appeal to, and rightfully demand the considerate attention of advanced teachers of truth; that through such relations he consciously receives knowledge, prepares for entrance to higher spheres, and better serves spirit in the circles of truth and righteousness.

For is not the lowest son of earth a spirit?

And if he is a spark of Divinity, even though dwelling upon the very outermost rim of the circle, in the midnight darkness, alone, separated for the time from the Great Light, in a universe of matter, not yet familiar with nor seemingly controlled by differentiated and understood laws, he will survive all changes and cataclysmic upheavals of nature, and finally emerge into conditions where, as spirit, he can and will assert the dignity of his origin, and the inherent powers of his divine attributes.

The wise will put no obstacle in the way of such.

There are many deep meanings and various interpretations to the words of the great Seer of Israel, "Suffer little children to come unto me and forbid them not."

The Christ, esoterically considered, is an individual as well as a cosmic possession, and it is the law that the individual spirit in conditions of weakness and ignorance, as well as in superior light may, if it so wills, receive recognition and spiritual instructions from those competent to impart knowledge.

That is destiny.

Upon earth men have established social orders and castes, which frequently subserve divine ends. I cannot criticise the wisdom of much that has been wrought into the various systems of government, and formulated by legislation. In their final results, conditions so created frequently lead to more desirable forms of civilization than had been previously attained, under the operation of preceding systems, even though the later and more modern expressions of the law have not always reflected the wisdom of sages nor involved highest forms of ethical teachings.

There are, in some respects, seemingly corresponding states of being in the celestial hierarchies. The former leaders in social states and caste, if they subserved the highest good of spirit in previous lives, are now rewarded in divine realization. If, however, they have not been so wise, they have indeed for the time placed millstones, so to speak, about their necks.

The gifts of the spirit—intuition, perception, consciousness and other allied attributes—are not useless possessions nor mockeries. They hold each and every one to strict accountability, and finally clothe their faithful votaries and servants in regal robes of beauty, indicative of acquired supremacy. In all conditions, absolute and equitable rewards and penalties follow.

All rulers, under whatever form of government, are equally subject to the unchanging law.

It is noticeable that as a spirit has thought, so has it become. Here pure thoughts have wrought spiritual revolutions, and now, as integral possessions of consciousness, have become efficient aids in the realization of sublime and useful wisdom. To those thus illuminated, the neophyte may appeal when desiring light upon matters of highest importance. Such, by virtue of superior wisdom, become guides and teachers to those seeking the truth. Fortunate, indeed, is he who attracts to his atmosphere the great expounders of the heavenly wisdom. Great also is the responsibility of the one who has obtained the light, for upon his teachings important issues depend.

Wonderful powers are attained only by those whose moral correspondences have prepared conditions for their proper exercise and control. But of the aspirants, or pupils? What of them? The hosts of Israel of old are said to have been fed upon manna from heaven. All under the broad canopies of the universe may receive spiritual manna, which shall not only become as meat and drink, but which also will enable partakers thereof to pass the boundaries of present knowledge and reach the planes of higher spiritual relation.

It largely depends upon the will to appropriate for spiritual benefit the teachings of the illuminati, and to learn through the lessons of experience the perfect and unchanging law, through the proper interpretation of which is conferred upon each one, sufficient light for the needs of the spirit in its various stages of realization.

The ultimate relations of the spirit to the law cannot be better illustrated by me than through a statement of the fact of the spirit's gradual unfoldment, with increased powers of receptivity, as occasions arise requiring further knowledge. Such necessities are perceived and special powers conferred, when the knowledge obtainable upon present planes of existence has been used, and served the purpose and end of being. It is the law that existing avenues of wisdom must first have been fully explored, leaving nothing of importance undiscovered, before the spirit obtains entrance to other and more extended horizons, where the expressions of the law appear in more sublimated forms, and the spirit, through clearer intuitions and perceptions, is able to evolve higher realizations than it had previously attained in lower states or spheres.

There is but one unchanging law, supreme in all the universe. The spirit in its evolution to different spheres of realization ever remains subject to it, though at times it may perceive new manifestations of its operation and learn that it has escaped the demands of the old and entered into a new state of being where it apparently has become a law unto itself. The spirit will, however, continue through each experience to learn more of the beautiful, synthetical relations in higher conditions of unending life than it had before comprehended—yet all will be but expressions of the supreme, unchanging cosmic order. Each step of the spirit's progress reveals clearer perceptions of harmony and celestial grandeur. Finally come the perfect revelations and manifestations of the law, completely justifying its existence and control in universal affairs. The reason accepts the issue. When this state has been attained, the spirit's exaltation has truly become a fact of being. Wonderful disclosures now wait upon it. An important victory has been won; new and better conditions and states prepared.

He who has achieved so much may go forth a messenger of light, teach much, influence many, finally binding his sheaves together in bands of love, claim them as evidence of faithful stewardship. Through such ministrations he comes into unity with the law and perceives its mode of expression.

Having now come to a clearer perception of the reasonableness and perfect justice of the law, and fully understanding that all were subject to its control, and that only by obedience to it could conditions pervaded by light and wisdom be realized, it seemed to me that my friends in spheres of humanity would readily accept the truths I might present.

That they would teach others from out the new and greater thesaurus seemed probable.

At first I could with difficulty control the thought vibrations, and from this cause, might without aid have failed in directing and concentrating upon any individual spirit.

Upon the larger plane of spiritual existence, what appears the natural condition and order everywhere prevailing, a part of the life, interwoven and inseparable from the universal spirit,—the eternal effluence,—cannot be wholly made available nor always clearly imparted as knowledge to the sons of earth, for the instruction and development of spirit. The methods of teaching which obtain in higher states of being are special, and beyond present mortal realization.

It is necessary for a spiritual teacher of humanity to synthesize, concentrate and aggregate the conglomerate, intellectual and spiritual forces, near to, and surrounding individual entities upon the plane of earth, bringing them into harmonial relations to more advanced spiritual states of being. Ultimately, perfect vibrations, through such means become operative, find their correspondences in sound, color, magnetic and electric auras, like to those emanating from higher spiritualized individualities.

It is possible to impress those in earthly forms through the medium of physical and psychical phenomena and counterparts.

Wisdom is, however, more frequently received through vibrations from spiritual spheres. Such appeals relate to highest capacities. Success in such efforts require that there shall be psychic and spiritual correspondences established between the subjective and objective intelligences. Under favorable conditions, the mortal mind may become the willing and useful instrument of the spirit. Some sensitives develop wonderful capacities in the ascending scale of spiritual realizations. The finer spiritual relations, however, are not fully realized until celestial correspondences obtain.

The higher revelations are possible only through the co-operation of those in spirit who, by their superior attainments, have acquired a perfect knowledge of the law of intercommunication. Such, by virtue of their wisdom, exercise the office of teachers, and control over many lower conditions.

The advanced illuminati are able to create psychic waves of great intensity, and through them reveal unto receptive minds a knowledge of the beautiful laws, through which spirit proclaims with unerring accuracy facts concerning the perfect wisdom, the infinite source, from which all intuitions and spiritual possessions are in essence derived and made to manifest divinity.

Equipped with sufficient understanding of the law and aided by the masters, any spirit may so control the powers and instrumentalities of the spiritual world as to enable it to reach and influence some one or more of those in earthly conditions, who can define forms of expression in both the material and spiritual states.

The measure of the value of teachings received by the mortal from such sources, correspond to the will, receptive capacity and uses to which they are applied. It principally depends upon the aspirant himself whether he receives the spiritual manna abundantly, and profits thereby, or in the recesses of his heart rejects the truth and becomes the vehicle of influences leading to disintegration, chaos and necessity of rebirth.

No one gains access to higher spheres except through obedience to the intuitions of the higher self which, properly defined, are modes of the law for individual guidance.

Correspondences to certain prevailing spiritual conditions is evidence of the spirit's present realization. There is, however, no limitation of its possibilities. Its present sphere is neither fixed nor permanent. It inherently possesses all the latent powers needful for the realization of perfect harmony. Methods may for the time seem to fail, but constant impressions received from higher sources will awaken aspiration, and lead the spirit out of bondage to material influences into light and freedom.

There is an aura indicating by its color and luminosity the spiritual correspondences to which one has attained. Its expressions are perceptible to adepts and seers. It is also, as it were, a means, clearer and more positive than any written hieroglyphics, how to estimate character, and becomes effectual for understanding how best to convey spiritual instruction. To some it may be needful that the lessons of physical phenomena, touching the feelings and finally awakening reason, should be taught, and to others through appeals made to higher psychical possessions. All approaches to the spirit, however, are but means to ends, and as such may be made to subserve beneficent purposes in the divine harmony. There are no set rules or methods of procedure.

Any spirit desirous of becoming a messenger of light and truth may elect or prescribe for itself such a course or method as may seem to it best designed to secure results, and in the final court of conscience, the wisdom of its selection and faithfulness of its stewardship will be revealed.

As previous possessions have prepared the spirit to teach, so may it hope to aid the realization of divinity in others. It is, however, always better for the neophyte to sit at the feet of a Gamaliel of wisdom until light is perceived, than to attempt the office of hierophant without sufficient preparation.

The vast armies of subalterns upon the plane of earth require for leaders the illuminati of the celestial spheres, nor are the great teachers unmindful of the needs of those in lower conditions of spirit. They come for highest good, and teach those in ignorance of the law's requirements, sublime truths.

Sensitive organisms of many of earth's children are employed by the great teachers for divine ends. They do not, however, require any one to blindly accept. They teach always to listen to the voice and judge by the results. They direct willing subjects and expound wisdom, which may be appropriated as an absolute possession of spirit.

The true light is a beacon unto all who come into the sphere of its influence, nor need a lesser luminary ever be mistaken for it. He who seeks co-operation with the great teachers of spiritual wisdom is never left in ignorance of the fact that the instructions he receives from them are for the purpose of the spirit's preparation to receive more direct impressions from the Infinite Source of all knowledge through his own intuitions. They always assert that they are but servants unto the Infinite. Other teachings should be distrusted and rejected.

The highest and most useful knowledge can never be exploited in the field of physical phenomena. Forms and the trance may subserve the temporary purpose of inciting investigation by the student. Some knowledge of the law of being may thereby be derived from those in higher spiritual correspondences, if such be the attraction, but the perfect understanding of truth is only attainable through individual consciousness and realization of the Infinite.

As each one is spirit, and experiences and states are always separate and individual, the highest correlations can only be established in the Infinite, where all expressions of the law are known and the necessity for every experience of the spirit clearly understood. This statement is logical and true. Being logical and true, and each one of earth a spirit, and a child of the Infinite, provisions exist for the acquirement of all needful knowledge, enabling the spirit to pass from the lower to higher states in its divine unfoldment; nor are the methods of procedure as shown for adoption to each individual consciousness of doubtful origin or value, but in perfect harmony with spiritual needs and powers of comprehension.

The cosmic idea of the destiny of the human race, with the power of reason to trace the origin and define the purpose of the law, has been revealed in consciousness to man only. He is in essence and practically as an objective fact to the subhuman kingdom, both a god and a mortal, for upon such planes he holds relation to it. Only through him has been revealed the supernal light, reflected in consciousness, as it were, from the very throne of the Infinite. He, old as time, true to the instincts and intuitions received at creation's dawn, has through all the ages, by struggles, conflicts, and trials infinite, illustrated the inherent supremacy of spirit, and proved himself a son of the Eternal Light.

When he shall have entered into the companionship of his elder brothers in spirit, received new lessons and revelations of the law, as expressed in its higher sublimations, mastered the details of duty, and perceived their full import, he will more clearly understand the necessity of all experiences through which he has passed. What his final destiny, no one who has traced his history along the thorny paths of experience can doubt. Heard he not the still, small voice in the beginning? Were not the eyes of his understanding open to the first scintillations of light? Did he not perceive some tones of harmony in apparent discord? Has he not already learned the first lessons in the order of self? Has he not established among his kind, at least, the partial recognition of his neighbor's right to his own? And does he not recognize the fact of yet much more to be accomplished in this direction? Is not such recognition an evidence of his divine origin? Has he not, under many names and in all climes, in sunshine and in darkest peril, supplicated the Infinite? Even in pre-historic times, walked he not as a king and ruler on the earth? Reason and analogy teach that he did so walk; in higher realms the fact is clearly perceived. While it is true that at times he has but dimly perceived his duty toward his kind, and strayed far from the light of the higher consciousness, yet, through the ministry of personal suffering, by war and physical death, he has been slowly taught the supremacy of the unchanging law, and gained admission to the higher realms of thought, and evolved clearer visions of what can be realized through obedience to the leadings of his diviner intuitions.

Though no two experiences have ever been the same, yet a knowledge of universal truth and harmony is slowly unfolding in the consciousness of man. He is learning to perceive that his neighbor in the bonds of ignorance is but a younger brother, a few centuries his junior, and that he will soon stand upon the plane of his present attainments, and appropriate for profitable use the vibrations of truth and love, now so highly prized by himself, while in conditions of higher realization he shall show him the path leading to the heights.

The Codes Of Hammurabi And Moses
W. W. Davies

QTY

The discovery of the Hammurabi Code is one of the greatest achievements of archaeology, and is of paramount interest, not only to the student of the Bible, but also to all those interested in ancient history...

Religion   **ISBN:** *1-59462-338-4*

Pages:132
MSRP $12.95

The Theory of Moral Sentiments
Adam Smith

QTY

This work from 1749. contains original theories of conscience amd moral judgment and it is the foundation for systemof morals.

Philosophy **ISBN:** *1-59462-777-0*

Pages:536
MSRP $19.95

Jessica's First Prayer
Hesba Stretton

QTY

In a screened and secluded corner of one of the many railway-bridges which span the streets of London there could be seen a few years ago, from five o'clock every morning until half past eight, a tidily set-out coffee-stall, consisting of a trestle and board, upon which stood two large tin cans, with a small fire of charcoal burning under each so as to keep the coffee boiling during the early hours of the morning when the work-people were thronging into the city on their way to their daily toil...

Pages:84

Childrens   **ISBN:** *1-59462-373-2*

MSRP $9.95

My Life and Work
Henry Ford

QTY

Henry Ford revolutionized the world with his implementation of mass production for the Model T automobile. Gain valuable business insight into his life and work with his own auto-biography... "We have only started on our development of our country we have not as yet, with all our talk of wonderful progress, done more than scratch the surface. The progress has been wonderful enough but..."

Pages:300

Biographies/   **ISBN:** *1-59462-198-5*

MSRP $21.95

www.bookjungle.com *email: sales@bookjungle.com fax: 630-214-0564 mail: Book Jungle PO Box 2226 Champaign, IL 61825*

The Art of Cross-Examination
Francis Wellman

QTY

I presume it is the experience of every author, after his first book is published upon an important subject, to be almost overwhelmed with a wealth of ideas and illustrations which could readily have been included in his book, and which to his own mind, at least, seem to make a second edition inevitable. Such certainly was the case with me; and when the first edition had reached its sixth impression in five months, I rejoiced to learn that it seemed to my publishers that the book had met with a sufficiently favorable reception to justify a second and considerably enlarged edition. ..

Reference   ISBN: *1-59462-647-2*

Pages:412

MSRP $19.95

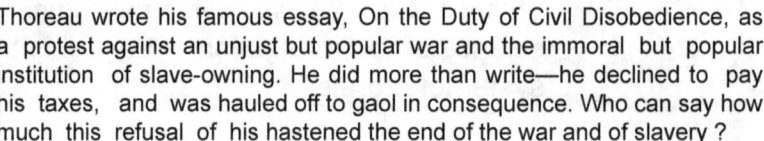

On the Duty of Civil Disobedience
Henry David Thoreau

QTY

Thoreau wrote his famous essay, On the Duty of Civil Disobedience, as a protest against an unjust but popular war and the immoral but popular institution of slave-owning. He did more than write—he declined to pay his taxes, and was hauled off to gaol in consequence. Who can say how much this refusal of his hastened the end of the war and of slavery ?

Law   ISBN: *1-59462-747-9*

Pages:48

MSRP $7.45

Dream Psychology
Psychoanalysis for Beginners

Sigmund Freud

Dream Psychology Psychoanalysis for Beginners
Sigmund Freud

QTY

Sigmund Freud, born Sigismund Schlomo Freud (May 6, 1856 - September 23, 1939), was a Jewish-Austrian neurologist and psychiatrist who co-founded the psychoanalytic school of psychology. Freud is best known for his theories of the unconscious mind, especially involving the mechanism of repression; his redefinition of sexual desire as mobile and directed towards a wide variety of objects; and his therapeutic techniques, especially his understanding of transference in the therapeutic relationship and the presumed value of dreams as sources of insight into unconscious desires.

Psychology   ISBN: *1-59462-905-6*

Pages:196

MSRP $15.45

The Miracle of Right Thought
Orison Swett Marden

QTY

Believe with all of your heart that you will do what you were made to do. When the mind has once formed the habit of holding cheerful, happy, prosperous pictures, it will not be easy to form the opposite habit. It does not matter how improbable or how far away this realization may see, or how dark the prospects may be, if we visualize them as best we can, as vividly as possible, hold tenaciously to them and vigorously struggle to attain them, they will gradually become actualized, realized in the life. But a desire, a longing without endeavor, a yearning abandoned or held indifferently will vanish without realization.

Self Help   ISBN: *1-59462-644-8*

Pages:360

MSRP $25.45

www.**bookjungle**.com *email: sales@bookjungle.com fax: 630-214-0564 mail: Book Jungle PO Box 2226 Champaign, IL 61825*

QTY

The Rosicrucian Cosmo-Conception Mystic Christianity by *Max Heindel*   ISBN: *1-59462-188-8*   **$38.95**
The Rosicrucian Cosmo-conception is not dogmatic, neither does it appeal to any other authority than the reason of the student. It is: not controversial, but is: sent forth in the, hope that it may help to clear...   New Age/Religion Pages 646

Abandonment To Divine Providence by *Jean-Pierre de Caussade*   ISBN: *1-59462-228-0*   **$25.95**
"The Rev. Jean Pierre de Caussade was one of the most remarkable spiritual writers of the Society of Jesus in France in the 18th Century. His death took place at Toulouse in 1751. His works have gone through many editions and have been republished...   Inspirational/Religion Pages 400

Mental Chemistry by *Charles Haanel*   ISBN: *1-59462-192-6*   **$23.95**
Mental Chemistry allows the change of material conditions by combining and appropriately utilizing the power of the mind. Much like applied chemistry creates something new and unique out of careful combinations of chemicals the mastery of mental chemistry...   New Age Pages 354

The Letters of Robert Browning and Elizabeth Barret Barrett 1845-1846 vol II
by *Robert Browning* and *Elizabeth Barrett*   ISBN: *1-59462-193-4*   **$35.95**
   Biographies Pages 596

Gleanings In Genesis (volume I) by *Arthur W. Pink*   ISBN: *1-59462-130-6*   **$27.45**
Appropriately has Genesis been termed "the seed plot of the Bible" for in it we have, in germ form, almost all of the great doctrines which are afterwards fully developed in the books of Scripture which follow...   Religion/Inspirational Pages 420

The Master Key by *L. W. de Laurence*   ISBN: *1-59462-001-6*   **$30.95**
In no branch of human knowledge has there been a more lively increase of the spirit of research during the past few years than in the study of Psychology, Concentration and Mental Discipline. The requests for authentic lessons in Thought Control, Mental Discipline and...   New Age/Business Pages 422

The Lesser Key Of Solomon Goetia by *L. W. de Laurence*   ISBN: *1-59462-092-X*   **$9.95**
This translation of the first book of the "Lernegton" which is now for the first time made accessible to students of Talismanic Magic was done, after careful collation and edition, from numerous Ancient Manuscripts in Hebrew, Latin, and French...   New Age/Occult Pages 92

Rubaiyat Of Omar Khayyam by *Edward Fitzgerald*   ISBN:*1-59462-332-5*   **$13.95**
Edward Fitzgerald, whom the world has already learned, in spite of his own efforts to remain within the shadow of anonymity, to look upon as one of the rarest poets of the century, was born at Bredfield, in Suffolk, on the 31st of March, 1809. He was the third son of John Purcell...   Music Pages 172

Ancient Law by *Henry Maine*   ISBN: *1-59462-128-4*   **$29.95**
The chief object of the following pages is to indicate some of the earliest ideas of mankind, as they are reflected in Ancient Law, and to point out the relation of those ideas to modern thought.   Religion/History Pages 452

Far-Away Stories by *William J. Locke*   ISBN: *1-59462-129-2*   **$19.45**
"Good wine needs no bush, but a collection of mixed vintages does. And this book is just such a collection. Some of the stories I do not want to remain buried for ever in the museum files of dead magazine-numbers an author's not unpardonable vanity..."   Fiction Pages 272

Life of David Crockett by *David Crockett*   ISBN: *1-59462-250-7*   **$27.45**
"Colonel David Crockett was one of the most remarkable men of the times in which he lived. Born in humble life, but gifted with a strong will, an indomitable courage, and unremitting perseverance...   Biographies/New Age Pages 424

Lip-Reading by *Edward Nitchie*   ISBN: *1-59462-206-X*   **$25.95**
Edward B. Nitchie, founder of the New York School for the Hard of Hearing, now the Nitchie School of Lip-Reading, Inc, wrote "LIP-READING Principles and Practice". The development and perfecting of this meritorious work on lip-reading was an undertaking...   How-to Pages 400

A Handbook of Suggestive Therapeutics, Applied Hypnotism, Psychic Science
by *Henry Munro*   ISBN: *1-59462-214-0*   **$24.95**
   Health/New Age/Health/Self-help Pages 376

A Doll's House: and Two Other Plays by *Henrik Ibsen*   ISBN: *1-59462-112-8*   **$19.95**
Henrik Ibsen created this classic when in revolutionary 1848 Rome. Introducing some striking concepts in playwriting for the realist genre, this play has been studied the world over.   Fiction/Classics/Plays 308

The Light of Asia by *sir Edwin Arnold*   ISBN: *1-59462-204-3*   **$13.95**
In this poetic masterpiece, Edwin Arnold describes the life and teachings of Buddha. The man who was to become known as Buddha to the world was born as Prince Gautama of India but he rejected the worldly riches and abandoned the reigns of power when...   Religion/History/Biographies Pages 170

The Complete Works of Guy de Maupassant by *Guy de Maupassant*   ISBN: *1-59462-157-8*   **$16.95**
"For days and days, nights and nights, I had dreamed of that first kiss which was to consecrate our engagement, and I knew not on what spot I should put my lips..."   Fiction/Classics Pages 240

The Art of Cross-Examination by *Francis L. Wellman*   ISBN: *1-59462-309-0*   **$26.95**
Written by a renowned trial lawyer, Wellman imparts his experience and uses case studies to explain how to use psychology to extract desired information through questioning.   How-to/Science/Reference Pages 408

Answered or Unanswered? by *Louisa Vaughan*   ISBN: *1-59462-248-5*   **$10.95**
Miracles of Faith in China   Religion Pages 112

The Edinburgh Lectures on Mental Science (1909) by *Thomas*   ISBN: *1-59462-008-3*   **$11.95**
This book contains the substance of a course of lectures recently given by the writer in the Queen Street Hall, Edinburgh. Its purpose is to indicate the Natural Principles governing the relation between Mental Action and Material Conditions...   New Age/Psychology Pages 148

Ayesha by *H. Rider Haggard*   ISBN: *1-59462-301-5*   **$24.95**
Verily and indeed it is the unexpected that happens! Probably if there was one person upon the earth from whom the Editor of this, and of a certain previous history, did not expect to hear again...   Classics Pages 380

Ayala's Angel by *Anthony Trollope*   ISBN: *1-59462-352-X*   **$29.95**
The two girls were both pretty, but Lucy who was twenty-one who supposed to be simple and comparatively unattractive, whereas Ayala was credited, as her Bombwhat romantic name might show, with poetic charm and a taste for romance. Ayala when her father died was nineteen...   Fiction Pages 484

The American Commonwealth by *James Bryce*   ISBN: *1-59462-286-8*   **$34.45**
An interpretation of American democratic political theory. It examines political mechanics and society from the perspective of Scotsman James Bryce   Politics Pages 572

Stories of the Pilgrims by *Margaret P. Pumphrey*   ISBN: *1-59462-116-0*   **$17.95**
This book explores pilgrims religious oppression in England as well as their escape to Holland and eventual crossing to America on the Mayflower, and their early days in New England...   History Pages 268

www.bookjungle.com *email: sales@bookjungle.com fax: 630-214-0564 mail: Book Jungle PO Box 2226 Champaign, IL 61825*

QTY

The Fasting Cure *by Sinclair Upton*   ISBN: *1-59462-222-1*   **$13.95**
*In the Cosmopolitan Magazine for May, 1910, and in the Contemporary Review (London) for April, 1910, I published an article dealing with my experi-
ences in fasting. I have written a great many magazine articles, but never one which attracted so much attention... New Age/Self Help/Health Pages 164*

Hebrew Astrology *by Sepharial*   ISBN: *1-59462-308-2*   **$13.45**
*In these days of advanced thinking it is a matter of common observation that we have left many of the old landmarks behind and that we are now pressing
forward to greater heights and to a wider horizon than that which represented the mind-content of our progenitors...   Astrology Pages 144*

Thought Vibration or The Law of Attraction in the Thought World   ISBN: *1-59462-127-6*   **$12.95**

by William Walker Atkinson   Psychology/Religion Pages 144

Optimism *by Helen Keller*   ISBN: *1-59462-108-X*   **$15.95**
*Helen Keller was blind, deaf, and mute since 19 months old, yet famously learned how to overcome these handicaps, communicate with the world, and
spread her lectures promoting optimism. An inspiring read for everyone...   Biographies/Inspirational Pages 84*

Sara Crewe *by Frances Burnett*   ISBN: *1-59462-360-0*   **$9.45**
*In the first place, Miss Minchin lived in London. Her home was a large, dull, tall one, in a large, dull square, where all the houses were alike, and all the
sparrows were alike, and where all the door-knockers made the same heavy sound...   Childrens/Classic Pages 88*

The Autobiography of Benjamin Franklin *by Benjamin Franklin*   ISBN: *1-59462-135-7*   **$24.95**
*The Autobiography of Benjamin Franklin has probably been more extensively read than any other American historical work, and no other book of its kind
has had such ups and downs of fortune. Franklin lived for many years in England, where he was agent...   Biographies/History Pages 332*

Name	
Email	
Telephone	
Address	
City, State ZIP	

☐ **Credit Card**   ☐ **Check / Money Order**

Credit Card Number	
Expiration Date	
Signature	

Please Mail to: Book Jungle
PO Box 2226
Champaign, IL 61825
or Fax to: 630-214-0564

ORDERING INFORMATION

web*: www.bookjungle.com*
email*: sales@bookjungle.com*
fax*: 630-214-0564*
mail*: Book Jungle PO Box 2226 Champaign, IL 61825*
or PayPal *to sales@bookjungle.com*

Please contact us for bulk discounts

DIRECT-ORDER TERMS

**20% Discount if You Order
Two or More Books**
Free Domestic Shipping!
Accepted: Master Card, Visa,
Discover, American Express